LEGEND-LED

THE STORY OF THE HOLY GRAIL.

LEGEND-LED

BY

AMY LE FEUVRE

AUTHOR OF 'PROBABLE SONS,' 'TEDDY'S BUTTON,' ETC.

LONDON

R·T·S-LUTTERWORTH PRESS

4, BOUVERIE STREET, E.C.4

Made in Great Britain
Printed by Purnell & Sons, Ltd.
Paulton (Somerset) and London

Contents

CHAPTER I

An Old Quest

IT was a very warm afternoon in July. In a front room with a large bay window overlooking the sea and beach at F—— were the three little Thurstons; and they were having their tea at a round table, presided over by their governess, Miss Gubbins. The atmosphere was close; the children's faces hot, and—if I may say it—sticky; and Miss Gubbins leant back in her chair fanning herself with a newspaper and watching her charges in lazy wonder, as they ate slice after slice of bread and butter, and emptied a large plate of prawns between them, talking ceaselessly as they did so.

Donald, the eldest, was a bright, handsome little fellow, who thought and acted for himself, and was generally in trouble through his independent spirit. Claud was fair and sturdy, had quite as strong a will as Donald, but was always willing to take advice; and Gypsy, as she was called, and whose proper name was Eleanor, was a quicksilvery, gentle-looking little maiden, with a fragile appearance and a spirit as high as either of her two brothers.

'A reg'lar handful!' pronounced the landlady, who had now had them as her lodgers for some years. 'The plagues of the terrace!' pronounced the two quiet maiden ladies next door.

'And the dearest children in the world when they're good,' Miss Gubbins would say.

Miss Gubbins took life very easily. She always dressed in grey, was very short-sighted, and had a passionate love for poetry, which love she tried to foster in her young charges. She was not a young woman, but had a simple freshness of mind and heart that always kept her in touch with children. Her rule was not a severe one, and except in the three hours of morning study, her little pupils were left very much to their own devices. Good principles she sought to instil into their minds, and beyond this she did not go.

She sat now, as she often did, listening to the conversation, but taking no part in it unless she was appealed to.

'Old Cole said he'd lend me some red paint, and I'll do it in letters large as life,' said Donald, with a little swagger in his tone.

'What will you put on it?' asked Claud thoughtfully, as he sucked a prawn's head and put it on the edge of his plate with a sigh, to think that he could get no more out of it.

'The resident's property.'

'What grand words!' And Gypsy opened her blue eyes to their widest extent.

'Trespassers will be prosecuted!' continued Donald.

What does prosecute mean?' asked Gypsy.

Burnt at the stake, and cut up in little pieces, and drowned, and arms and legs twisted off, and eyes put out with red hot pokers!' said Claud with cheerful assurance.

'That's persecuted, you booby!'

Donald's tone was contemptuous. He added, 'And if that won't keep the visitors off our corner, I'll fight every one of them !'

'You wouldn't beat them. You might the mother's children, but not the nursery ones, nor the school-room ones ; and there are two sets of school-room ones coming to-morrow, the Stevens, and the Burkes who were here last year !'

'I shall get old Cole to help me.'

'And I'll help you too, and I'll put on my boots, because the kicks will hurt more !'

This was from Gypsy, whose eyes sparkled in anticipation of a coming contest. Then Miss Gubbins spoke.

'What are you all talking about ? Don't let me hear of you fighting any one !'

'Well, it's our bit of beach, it has got the big rock on it, and the longest breakwater, and we're residents, aren't we, Gubby ? And the visitor children aren't going to drive us from it—two boys tried it on this afternoon—and we'll let them know who we are !'

Donald spoke excitedly, and flourished his tea-cup in his hand like a war club.

'And they were only nursery children, too !' cried Claud with scorn.

'I don't understand what you mean by "nursery children,"' said Miss Gubbins.

'Oh, Gubby, you know ! We told you the other day ; they are the ones that live in a nursery, of course. All the children that come here belong to three lots. The school-room ones come with their governess or from school ; they're the jolliest. Some of the nursery ones aren't bad, but the nurses are horrid, and the mother's children are worst of all !

They have company manners and best frocks and kid gloves, and always live in the drawing-room!'

Miss Gubbins smiled.

Donald went on : ' And the residents always come first, before the visitors. The beach belongs to us in the winter, and we aren't going to give up our pet corner in the summer for any wretched little visitor!'

'You will not be residents here much longer,' said Miss Gubbins, rousing herself; 'I am only waiting till you have done tea to tell you about it. I heard from your step-brother this morning.'

There were shouts at this. ' The Ogre!' 'Is he coming to see us?' 'What did he say?'

Miss Gubbins would not satisfy any curiosity until the tea things were removed, hands and faces washed, and a tidy little group gathered round her. The children were always curious when there was any correspondence between Victor Thurston and their governess. He was almost a stranger to them. He had been abroad when his father had married a young wife, and never saw the children till after their mother's death, which occurred when Gypsy was born. Then he came home for a few months, as his father was taken ill, and followed his second wife to the grave within six months of her death. Victor made arrangements for the children to be taken to Miss Gubbins, who was a friend of their mother, and she had come into rooms with them at the sea-side, where they had remained ever since. And then Victor had gone abroad again, and, beyond a short visit one summer, during which he inspired the children with the greatest awe, he had not been near them.

'Do tell us, Gubby, quick!' pleaded Claud. 'Is he coming here?'

'No, but we are going to him. Now don't scream so, and I will tell you. An uncle of yours has died, and has left your brother an old house in the country. He says it is too large for him to live in alone, and he wants us to go there at once.'

'The Ogre's Castle! Hip, hip, hurrah! Are we going to-morrow?'

'The end of next week.'

'And is he there?'

'No, he will not come till a month later, he says.'

'Then we shall do just as we like, and you'll give us a holiday, like a dear good Gubby, won't you?'

'I shall see.'

'Do tell us what it is like, and if there are dungeons, and secret rooms?'

'I know nothing about it. Now, you mustn't worry me with questions, but have patience, for we shall soon be there.'

There was much excitement about the coming change; but, when they had quieted down, Miss Gubbins told them she would read to them as usual, as the tide was in, and they could not go out on the beach. This was a custom of hers nearly every evening, and she had been half telling, half reading, Tennyson's thrilling tale of King Arthur and his knights.

To-night she chose the 'Holy Grail,' and, mystical as it was, the little ones' shining eyes and rapt attention told her how much they had enjoyed it.

They drew long breaths when she finished.

'And Galahad never came back,' said Claud, dreamily looking out to the sunset sky across the bay. 'It's rather sad, but it's lovely!'

'I shouldn't like to be too good,' said Donald meditatively; 'that's what people mean when they say some children are too good to live. They're afraid of being caught away like Sir Galahad!'

Gypsy said nothing. She sat with clasped hands on a footstool, her pretty little face unusually grave. In her small heart she was saying to herself, 'I wish I could find it. I should like to start to-morrow!'

'It's only a story, you know, children; but every one in this world is seeking for something, and it is only to some that special blessing is given. We all ought to try for it.'

'Try for what?' asked Donald.

'Well,' said Miss Gubbins vaguely, 'try to be very, very good, like Galahad. He went through the world looking for heavenly glory, and he found it.'

'I think I'd rather be like Lancelot,' said Donald. 'He wasn't quite so very good as Galahad. Gubby, do you think there will be a big hall and a round table in the Ogre's Castle?'

The conversation drifted away from the old legends to the near future, and little Gypsy was the only one of the three who went to bed that night with her brain full of stormy seas, golden light, and boats of fire riding on the waves. When Miss Gubbins bent over her the last thing at night, she caught the murmured words, 'I see the boat; it's coming for me!'

The next day found the children on the beach—not quite so keen upon having the sole monopoly of their favourite corner, now that they knew they were going away. They soon made their little companions aware of the fact, and talked rather grandly about the 'castle' they were going to live in. They were busily employed with others in laying out gardens in the sand, with seaweed lawns, pebble paths, and miniature lakes, when Gypsy felt herself pulled by the hand. Turning round, she met the earnest gaze of a little girl about her own age, evidently a new-comer.

'May I play with you?' was the shy request.

Then Gypsy proceeded with the usual catechism to which all new-comers were subjected.

'What's your name?'

'Irene Gordon.'

'Have you got a governess?'

'No.'

'A mother?'

'Mother is in London with father.'

'Have you got a nurse?'

'Yes; she's over there with my little baby brother.'

'You can come and get some crabs to put in the lake with me.'

And Gypsy led her off in a grandmotherly fashion.

Irene was a pale, uninteresting-looking child, but Gypsy's frank conversation soon put her at ease, and she gave her her full confidence.

'I came here the day before yesterday. I saw you playing, and wanted to come so much, but I didn't like to. You make much better castles and gardens than any one else!'

'That's because we're—we're residers,' said Gypsy, struggling with the long word.

'I never have any one to play with at home,' continued Irene with a sigh; 'and I'm always being punished, and no one loves me.'

'You must be a wicked girl, then!' and Gypsy stopped in her operation of turning over stones to find some crabs, and regarded her new friend with doubtful eyes.

'Nurse says I am. I don't like nurse, and she doesn't like me.'

'Nurses are very nasty, I think. We haven't a nurse, only Gubby, and she's very nice. But we haven't a father and mother, like you. Don't they like you?'

Irene did not answer for a minute, then she said slowly,—

'I'm a kind of mistake, you know. I don't know how I came, but I was born wrong. I ought to have been a boy, and mother doesn't like girls. Father said, when Percy was born, that he was worth a dozen girls, for he was the heir. I don't quite understand what a heir is. I know he will have our house when he grows up, and I shan't have nothing! No one wants me at home. If I only knew some one who did, I would run away to them; but then, that's rather a frightening thing to do!'

'It would be lovely,' said Gypsy, with sparkling eyes. 'You could have all kinds of adventures if you ran away. You could sleep in the woods—climb up a tree when night came, because of the wolves, and eat berries and rabbits, and boil a kettle, and—and join a circus, and be dressed in gold and silver, and jump through hoops, and have all the people clapping you, and then you'd grow up a rich lady, and marry a prince, and live in a castle ever after!'

Irene listened to this burst of eloquence much impressed.

'But where should I find a circus?'

'Oh, they're always just outside the wood in story-books. Or you could be like Galahad, and go riding after the "Holy Thing."'

'Who was she ? '

'It was a man, not a she. He was very, very good. And a lot of knights rode away one day to find it.'

'Find what ? '

'The Holy Thing.'

'What's that ? '

'Well, it was a kind of glory light, something like a cup all in red and yellow and silver. It came from heaven to only very good people, and they all went to find it, and Galahad did. He went across the sea on bridges, and there was an awful storm, and he wouldn't stop for nobody or nothing, and at last a little boat took him right into the sky, and he never came back again.'

'And what did he see in the sky ? '

Gypsy considered ; then in a solemn tone she replied, 'God.'

'I don't think I'll be like that,' said Irene gravely. ' That would be a frightening journey.'

'Well, I'm going to go one day. I shall set out and find it, and then I shall never come back.'

'Hi! Gypsy, hurry up! Where are the crabs ? '

It was Donald, who was waxing impatient ; and the little girls dropped their conversation for the present.

CHAPTER II

Trying to Find

'LITTLE girl, would you like to come and have some singing with us?'

It was a young lady who spoke to Gypsy the next afternoon, as she was walking disconsolately along the beach, wishing it was not Sunday, that she might have a good romp with her brothers. They were lying down under a bathing machine, busy with some books with which Miss Gubbins had provided them. Gypsy could not read well, and she had looked at pictures till she was tired, so she glanced up brightly when spoken to.

'Yes, I'll come. I like to sing.'

She followed her guide to a quiet little corner under the cliffs, where about a dozen boys and girls were assembled. And in a few minutes some bright hymns were started, and then the young lady began to talk to them.

A great deal was unintelligible to Gypsy, but the subject was the 'Pearl of greatest price,' and Miss Pringle, who was talking, gave them the story of a pearl from the time it was first formed in an oyster-shell to the time it was sold to merchants, and cleaned and set in rings and jewelry of all sorts. Then she told them of the one pearl that was really worth finding, and she concluded by making them each repeat after her the little verse, 'I love them that love Me, and those that seek Me early shall find Me.'

When it was all over, and Gypsy was moving away, she put her hand on her shoulder.

'Are you going to seek for the pearl of greatest price, little one?'

Gypsy knit her brows in thought.

'What is it?' she asked. 'Is it the Holy G'ail?'

'It is Jesus Christ Himself. He loves you, and asks you to come to Him. Make up your mind to seek Him, dear, and you will find Him!'

She turned to some others, and Gypsy crept away, her little mind strangely confused between a pearl, a cup in the midst of golden light, and the Lord Himself; but one thing she was determined on, and that was that she would search until she found.

'I've been to a kind of Sunday-school,' she announced to her brothers, a short time after.

'Where?'

'Round the corner over there. A nice lady told us a story of a man who was looking about everywhere for pearls. At last he found a lovely big one, only it cost a dreadful lot of money. Then he thought he must have it, so he went home and sold all his things, and came back with the money and bought it.'

'And what did he do with it?'

'He never let it go. He kept it. He was like Galahad looking for the Holy Thing. He found it after a long, long time, but it cost a lot of money.'

'Galahad found the Holy Grail without paying for it.'

'Yes, I'd rather see that than a pearl,' said Gypsy wistfully. 'I'm going to be very, **very** good when

B

we go away from here, and perhaps I shall find it in the old house we're going to.'

'I think,' said Donald, regarding his sister curiously, 'that you can't be good more than two days. That's the longest I can. But what I mean to try is to be good all the week till the last day, and then I'll just be as wicked as ever I can, to keep me from bursting.'

This resolve rather staggered Claud and Gypsy.

'And what will be your wicked day?' asked Claud. Donald considered.

'Saturday, I think, because I can begin quite fresh on Sunday.'

'But I expect Sunday will be quite a busy day with punishing you,' said Claud gravely; 'and if the Ogre is with us, he'll punish you worse than Gubby!'

'It's very wicked to mean to be wicked,' said Gypsy, with serious, solemn eyes.

'Don't be a little prig, and you needn't preach, because you're always in mischief, and you'll never find the Holy Thing, if you live to be a thousand years old!'

'I shall,' said Gypsy tearfully. 'You're a horrid boy, and I shan't tell you nothing about it when I do find it.'

She left the boys, and went to find Miss Gubbins, who read aloud to her for a little; but though Gypsy told her about the Sunday class, her own resolve was kept locked up in her little heart, and Miss Gubbins had no idea of the effect of the poem upon the impressionable child.

Irene Gordon was the recipient of Gypsy's confidences. She followed her about the beach like a little shadow, and the two became great friends. The boys liked the little stranger because 'she didn't give herself airs.' In other words, she would fetch and carry for them without a murmur, and when Gypsy urged her to rebel against their autocratic rule, she looked quite astonished.

'Boys always must be waited on, mustn't they? Girls are nobodies!'

When the last day came, and the little Thurstons ran here and there on the beach saying good-bye to all their little friends and acquaintances, Irene came up to Gypsy and sobbed aloud:

'I wish you weren't going away; I shall never see you again. Couldn't you take me with you? I'm so dull at home!'

'I'm 'fraid we might be took up by the police if we stole you,' said Gypsy, putting her little arms round Irene's neck and giving her an affectionate hug. 'But I think you had really better run away, if no one wants you at home, and perhaps I may meet you on a high hill one day, and we'll both be looking for —for what I told you about!'

'I should be so frightened,' murmured Irene.

'Oh no, you wouldn't! I'm never frightened when I'm taking a walk. And if you get into a storm, ask God to take care of you. I always do.'

They parted, and Irene was only half comforted; but she went back to her nurse and baby brother, and Gypsy and her brothers took their last farewell of their beloved beach, and were soon in the train with Miss Gubbins, having closed the first chapter in their life.

Poor Miss Gubbins was thankful when the journey was ended. The children's high spirits at first were difficult to contend with; then they grew tired and cross, and quarrelling commenced, so she had to assert her authority to preserve peace. They reached a quiet little country station at last about six o'clock in the evening ; and when they got out on the platform they found they were the only passengers that alighted there. The station-master came bustling up to them, and informed them that the carriage was waiting outside. And they found a comfortable, though rather shabby brougham, with two very fat, sleek horses, and an old coachman, who looked quite aghast at the luggage.

He got off the box, and shook his head remonstratingly. 'Now, now, this is too much to expec' my horses to drag eight miles ! Should say, if my 'pinion was axed, that a box each, size according to size, would a been all that was desired, and here's three monsters, and a hamper, and three little 'uns, not to speak of a few band-boxes, and such like as females have a likin' to ! I never would have in the missus's time more than I thought fit to carry, and 'tisn't to be expected——'

'My good man,' said Miss Gubbins a little shortly, 'take what luggage you can, and leave the rest. It must either be sent up from the station, or you must come down again for it. Don't let us waste time talking about it !'

The old man looked at her in astonishment, but something in Miss Gubbins' manner made him alter his behaviour. Grumblingly he turned to the luggage, and with the help of the porters got some of it stowed away on the carriage, the station-master promising to send the rest up in a cart that could be lent for that purpose. And then the children bundled in, and with a tired sigh Miss Gubbins resigned herself to the long drive.

'Where's the sea?' asked Claud, after he had got tired of looking out at the narrow green lanes through which they were passing.

'I don't think there will be any sea here,' said Miss Gubbins. 'I told you I thought there would be none.'

'But there's some kind of water somewhere,' said Donald.

'I don't know ; sit still, and wait to see.'

The drive was over at last. They came to a lodge-gate, which was opened by a pleasant-looking woman —the old coachman's wife—and as he drove in he called out : 'Oh yes, they've come safe and sound, and a deal more of them than is wanted in this part !'

'What a rude old man !' said Donald. 'I'll fight him, if he talks like that to me !'

'Hush, Donald. I think I had better tell you that your brother wrote to me saying there were some very old servants here, who had quite managed the house when your uncle got very old. We must all be polite to them, and not take any notice of their remarks till your brother comes. And I wish,' Miss Gubbins added, with a little sigh, 'that he were here now.'

When the house was reached, the children looked at it with delight and awe. It was an old Elizabethan building in red brick, with projecting gables and case-ment windows. When they got inside, they found themselves in a large entrance hall wainscoted in old oak, a broad wooden staircase leading up to a gallery above from the centre of the hall.

'I am sure,' whispered Claud, in awe to his brother, 'that this was where King Arthur and his knights lived.'

'Yes,' responded Donald delightedly. 'Look at

their armour and swords hanging up on the walls!'

A very important-looking old lady in a black silk dress received them, and the children thought the house belonged to her until Miss Gubbins told them she was the housekeeper, and her name was Mrs. Peck. She had a nice tea prepared for them in the large dining-room.

'I'm sure I don't know what rooms to give you,' she said to Miss Gubbins, 'but I've done my best. There's a set of rooms upstairs which will suit you, I think. One is the old nursery—at least it was fifty year ago—and it's a nice sunny room, and there's a bedroom leading into it that I thought would do for you and the little girl, and another room on the same landing for the two little boys. We haven't had children in this house for forty years, and most of the rooms are shut up. When Mr. Thurston comes back he will say what he wishes. But these three rooms will be quite enough for you till he comes, I should think.'

'Certainly,' said Miss Gubbins brightly. 'We will go and look at them after tea.'

'But we shall use all the rooms in the house if we like,' said Donald, looking at Mrs. Peck defiantly. 'We had three rooms where we came from, and we aren't babies, to be put in a nursery!'

'Hush, Donald! that is not the way to speak. Go on with your tea.'

Mrs. Peck said nothing, but her gaze encountered Donald's, and from that time it was war to the knife between them.

After tea they all went up the old staircase, along the gallery, until they came to a side wing of the house, and here were the rooms prepared for them. The nursery was a large room, with a deep window-seat, and two cupboards in the recesses on each side of the fireplace.   A table in the middle of the room, a horsehair sofa, one arm-chair, and six old-fashioned wooden ones with rush seats, formed the furniture of it.   There were no pictures on the walls, and the carpet was threadbare and shabby, as were also some faded crimson curtains to the window.

'Quite suitable for children,' said Mrs. Peck, as she noticed Miss Gubbins' downcast face.

'We will soon make it bright and comfortable,' said Miss Gubbins.

'It smells nasty,' said Gypsy critically, 'but it will be a lovely room to play in.'

'The table isn't round,' said Donald, inspecting it.

'That's dreadful,' said Claud.   'We can't be Arthur's knights here.'

Then they went into the bedrooms, but the children did not take much interest in them, and soon came back to the old nursery.

'I love the window,' said Gypsy, climbing upon the window-seat, and trying to open the casement. 'Look how high up we are!   We can see for miles and miles, and there's no sea anywhere.'

'What are these horrid bars outside the window?' said Claud, with a disgusted face, as he tried to lean out of it.

'I tell you what it is,' said Donald, in an eager excited whisper, 'the Ogre has told Mrs. Peck to put us in here, and then he's going to lock us in, and we shall be in prison.   Castles always have prisons up-stairs as well as dungeons.'

'How shall we get anything to eat?' enquired Gypsy, looking as if she rather liked the prospect.

'Oh, the food will come up in baskets outside the window, and we shall pull it up by a rope.'

'What fun!'

'And,' continued Claud, who would never be outdone in imagination by his brother, 'every day there'll be a little less to eat, until at last one slice of bread and butter will come up, and we shall have to divide it between us, and it will have to last the whole day!'

'And then what?'

'And then there will be none,' said Donald, in a tragic voice.

Their conversation was interrupted here by Miss Gubbins coming in and taking them off to bed; and by this time they were so tired and sleepy, that they were only too glad to obey.

The next morning Gypsy woke up very early. The sun was streaming into the bedroom, and she looked round the room curiously, for Miss Gubbins was still asleep, and she knew she must keep quiet. She noticed the quaint, old-fashioned furniture, and thought it much nicer than the modern kind they were accustomed to in their seaside lodgings, and then she started, as she saw on the wall opposite her, a dingy, faded-looking text in a frame with these words upon it—

'Those that seek Me early shall find Me.'

'Why, that's the text that lady gave me to learn,' she said to herself; and then her thoughts rambled in this fashion:

'She said it was Jesus I must look for. I wonder if I shall find Him here. It's much more likely in a great old house like this, than in those old lodgings.

" Seek Me early." Then it's early in the morning, like this, when I ought to look for Him. I 'spect it's only to very, very good people He shows Himself. And He'll be in a beautiful golden light. Oh, I should like to see Him for a little tiny minute, and then I would know He was pleased with me. I wish I could find Him, and wouldn't the boys be 'stonished when I told them! I wonder if I've been good enough. I've been trying hard to be like Galahad. I didn't hit Claud when he pinched me in the train, and I only called him a " silly" once, I didn't call him a " beast," and I'm sure he was one! And then I kissed that horrid cook when we came away, and I didn't say " No " like the boys when she asked me to. I s'pose it will be very hard and difficult to find Jesus, but Galahad saw the Holy Thing in front of him all the way. If I could only once see a little bit of it, I should be so glad—I will try! I will get up now, because it's early, and it's very quiet like Sunday, and I'll creep along these big old passages, and peep into all the rooms. " Those that seek Me early shall find Me." Jesus said that, so it must be true, and p'r'aps I shall find Him this very morning!'

She lay still pondering over the text with big eyes, and at last stole quietly out of the bedroom in her dressing gown and little slippers.

Along the gallery she crept, trying the handle of every door as she did so ; but most of them were locked. A few rooms were open, and from the threshold she regarded the large fourpost bedsteads, with heavy hangings, the shrouded furniture, and the darkened windows with a doubtful awe. There seemed a great many passages, and at last disappointment crept into her little heart.

' I'd better go back, I don't like these dark rooms. I shall never find Jesus here!'

She was just turning back, when she saw at the end of the narrow passage in which she was, a door just ajar, and light streaming out. This looked more promising, but when she crept up, and pushed the heavy door open, she caught her breath in delight and astonishment. Had she come after all to the right place?

CHAPTER III

Almost Successful

IT was not a bedroom she was in now. A room with dark panelled walls and ceiling, with rows upon rows of books stretching from floor to roof, a table in the centre of the room, with great carved corners and legs; and as Gypsy looked, she thought she saw hideous creeping creatures crawling over it, and making faces at her; some heavy chairs, and smaller tables in deep recesses. But this was not what entranced her eye. Opposite her, taking up the whole of one side of the room, was a stained glass window, and Gypsy felt at once this must be a kind of church.

She looked up in expectation, and then the thought came into her mind: 'I'd better say my prayers, and then I can ask God to help me find Jesus.'

She knelt down, a little figure with tumbled golden curls, and a wistful, dreamy little face; and as she knelt she prayed:

'O God—I thank Thee for taking care of me all night, and please take care of me to-day. Make me a good girl, and forgive me for being naughty, and bless Gubby, and Donald, and Claud, and take us all to heaven when we die——'

Thus far she got very easily, for it was her usual morning prayer, but she wanted something more to-day, and after a long pause she added, in an awed whisper : 'And please, God, help me to find Jesus now. I'd like to find Him here, because I've got up early, as He told me. For Jesus Christ's sake— Amen.' She knelt on in silence for a minute with tightly closed eyes, and then she opened them, and the morning sun having just found its way in at the window, streamed through the coloured glass in rays of red, blue, and yellow, upon the very spot of floor in front of her.

The child looked up in delighted wonder and content. Yes, the lovely light was coming down to her just like it did to Galahad, and God was answering her prayer already. She had found the 'Holy Thing' at last. She gazed and gazed, hoping to see something more ; she put out her little hands, and let the coloured sunbeams play over them, she moved on her knees a step forward, and shook out her white woollen dressing gown in the golden light, and with a smile of perfect content she looked up to the roof and said aloud : 'Thank you very much, God, it's lovely, it's just what I thought Galahad saw, but please let me see Jesus Himself just a minute. I know He must be here.'

But she saw nothing more, and after a time she got up from her knees, for the sun had gone behind a cloud, and the beautiful rays had vanished ; and with a little child's sublime faith she trotted away, saying to herself :

'God did hear me, and I'll come another day and find Jesus. Perhaps He has gone somewhere else to-day, but I know I'll find Him here, because of the beautiful light.'

When outside in the dark passages, she felt quite

bewildered, and after vainly trying to find her way back to the bedroom, she sat down and relieved her over-wrought little brain by a burst of tears.

'And now I'm lost, or perhaps, as I've seen the holy light, I'm not to go back to Gubby and the boys, and they'll never find me again—like Galahad! But, oh, I do want to get back to bed—and—and I'm very hungry!'

She was sobbing away, when a maid appeared, and stared at her as if she had been a small ghost.

'Sakes alive! How you scared me! However did you come a wanderin' over here? There, bless your little heart, don't cry! I'm Jane as brought you your bath-water last night. Don't you remember me? Let me carry you back to your guv'ness. What's she thinkin' of, to let you wander out o' your bed in this fashion? But there, I never did hold with guv'nesses; little mites like you ought to have a nurse, and not be havin' your brains stuffed to burstin' with jography and sums, and such outlandish things!'

Muttering which, Jane picked her up like a baby, and astonished poor sleepy Miss Gubbins by depositing her on her bed.

Gypsy was too excited and tired to explain where she had been, and Miss Gubbins could only conjecture that she had walked in her sleep, so she tucked her up in her own little bed again, and Gypsy went soundly to sleep, and never woke till Miss Gubbins was up and dressed, and waiting to begin her toilet. Gypsy was rather quiet over the nursery breakfast. The boys were in the highest spirits, and were longing to tear all over the house, but Miss Gubbins gave them a little lecture before they left her wing.

'I shall be very busy this morning unpacking, and I want you all to be very good. Remember the old servants here have never been accustomed to children, and I think they do not like the idea of our coming at all. Show them that you can be polite and gentle, and don't let them think I have brought you up like little savages.'

'As long as old Peck doesn't come near us we shall do,' said Donald.

And then, after promising they would not get into mischief, away they went.

'It's lovely to have such a large house to live in,' said Claud; 'what splendid fun we shall have when we play hide and seek!'

'Yes, but it's a shame all the rooms are locked up! Let us come downstairs into the garden.'

They found their way out, and for the next couple of hours were enjoying themselves thoroughly, in running along an old flower garden, laid out in terraces; then down on the velvet lawns, and through the shrubberies; and finally finding their way to the walled kitchen garden, with glass houses of grapes, and melons, and fruit and vegetables in abundance.

'It's like a fairy palace,' said Gypsy, as after coaxing and wheedling the old gardener in charge to give them some fruit, they threw themselves down under a shady beech on the lawn, and proceeded to enjoy some fallen apples, six ripe plums, and a rhubarb leaf full of raspberries.

'Yes,' said Donald contentedly; 'it isn't much like an ogre's castle, is it?'

'Does "Agony" live here?' asked Gypsy.

Donald nodded his head and looked very wise.

'She was talking to me this morning; she's getting

angry, and we shall have to do something to please her to-day, or to-night she'll be awful. You see that lot of bushes over there? we shall have to crawl through them on our hands and knees directly after dinner to-day!'

Gypsy's face lengthened, and Claud said, dismally, 'One of those bushes is made of holly; we shall bleed to death!'

'Well, we must do it, and I'm always the first one to go through!'

To explain this conversation, I must tell you that 'Agony' was a mysterious game that the children invented, and that was always being played. Gypsy more than half believed it was true. Agony' was supposed to be a very hard and cruel spirit who lived with them always, and was constantly requiring them to do dreadful things to appease her wrath. Donald was chief inventor, and held the game in his own hands, for he was the priest, and dictated 'Agony's' wishes to his younger brother and sister. 'Agony' appeared in the shape of smoke or steam—if a steamer or train passed the children at the seaside, their one idea was to look at the smoke. If it came puffing out in great white wreaths, 'Agony' was in a good temper, but if the smoke was black, she was angry, and some painful exploit must be attempted at once to soothe her anger. Sometimes Claud and Gypsy would wax rebellious, and refuse to do what Donald ordained, then at night they knew what to expect. A figure in a white sheet would creep out at them from behind some dark corner on the stairs, or crawl out from under their beds, and Gypsy would invariably succumb at once. 'Don't come near me, Agony, oh please don't! I will be good, I will, I promise you!' And if Claud squared his shoulders and with clenched fists prepared for combat, he was quite certain to get the worst of it, so they both learnt that rebellion was useless.

Now Gypsy asked curiously :

'Where shall we see Agony, Don ? There are no trains or steamers here. P'raps she won't be here at all, and we shall get rid of her for ever.'

'Oh,' said Donald, who was never at a loss, 'you'll see her fast enough. She will come out of the chimneys here.'

Gypsy looked disappointed.

'And,' pursued Donald, with a sudden inspiration, 'if she isn't pleased after we've crawled through those bushes this afternoon, we shall have to crawl down the staircase from top to bottom on our hands six times !'

'This is a lovely staircase for that,' said Claud, adding with guile, 'Don't you think Agony would like us to slide down on the banisters ? We couldn't do it at the lodging, because they had so many corners, but we could here.'

And then Gypsy said very slowly :

'I sha'n't do it if it's naughty, because I'm going to be very, very good always. I saw something this morning that you haven't seen.'

'What ?'

'I saw'—Gypsy paused, and shook her head from side to side with great solemnity—'I saw the Holy Thing !'

'You're a wicked story-teller !'

'I'm not. I did see it. I got up very early to look for it, and I went along the passages, and opened some doors, and after a long, long time I saw a door a little bit open, and I went in, and there was a lovely church window, and it was a dark room with hundreds and thousands of books—the walls were made of books—and I knelt down on the carpet, and after I had said my prayers I opened my eyes, and— and there it was.'

'What was it like?' asked Donald sceptically, whilst Claud gazed at his little sister with open mouth and eyes.

'It was a lovely glory light, red, and yellow, and blue, and it came right down upon me, and made me all red and blue and yellow too, and it stayed a few minutes, and then it went away.'

'Show us the room, and we will believe you,' said Donald, still unbelieving, but the sweet seriousness of Gypsy's face almost making him waver.

'Why didn't you tell us before?' asked Claud.

'Because I was waiting to tell it when you weren't too busy.'

And then Gypsy trotted into the house, and the boys followed her. Such a search they had, up and down stairs and along every passage; but though they opened the doors of many rooms, the particular one could not be found.

'We knew you were telling stories,' said Donald triumphantly, and Gypsy with tears in her eyes protested again and again that she was speaking the truth.

'Well, if the room was here before breakfast it is here now,' said Donald sternly, 'and if you can't find it, it will be all a make up. I knew you weren't good enough to find the Holy Thing!'

'I lost my way coming back,' sobbed Gypsy, 'and Jane found me and carried me back to bed; you ask

c

her if she didn't. I did see the Holy Thing. I don't care what you say. I did, I did!'

'Hulloo, let's come down this staircase,' exclaimed Claud, opening a door that looked like a cupboard, 'here are a lot more rooms here, and here's one with the door unlocked.'

He bounced in, and then stopped in consternation; it was Mrs. Peck's private sitting-room, and she was having a slight lunch, consisting of a glass of wine and some cake which looked very tempting.

She stood up when she saw them, and bristled all over with anger and annoyance.

'Now, once for all, I'll have you children to understand that you'll keep to your own rooms, and not be prying and peeping into rooms that don't belong to you—such impertinence! Without a knock, or if you please—bursting into my private room, which the old master himself never would presume to enter!'

'You've got the comfortablest room in the house,' said Donald, standing at the door and looking round with cool unconcern.

'I say, Mrs. Peck, tell us, is there a room like a church in this house? Gypsy says there is, and we know she's humbugging.'

'I'm not, I'm speaking true; there is a beautiful window in it, isn't there, Mrs. Peck?'

Poor Gypsy eagerly waited for Mrs. Peck's answer. If she could only get some one to tell the boys that she was right!

But Mrs. Peck swept them all out of the room. 'I don't know what your guv'ness is for, if she can't keep you from tearing all over the house in this fashion. A room like a church! Thank goodness we've none of that sort here. A popish chapel maybe you're expecting? There, go along, and never let me see you in my part of the house again!'

'There!' cried the boys in triumph to the discomfited Gypsy, 'of course we knew you were telling stories; come on, old Peck is a horrid old thing; we'll go and find Gubby and see what she is doing.'

Away they tore, but Gypsy followed more slowly. Was it possible it had been all a dream, she wondered? Her little mind was sorely perplexed, and she wandered off again by herself down the passages to see if she could find the room. It was all in vain, and she came to her early dinner with a sad and downcast little face.

The boys had no mercy on her.

'Fancy, Gubby, Gypsy has been trying to make us believe she saw the Holy Thing. She vowed she went into a room and saw it before breakfast. And when we asked her to show us the room, she says she can't find it. The room has disappeared! Very wonderful, isn't it?'

'Ha, ha!' laughed Claud, 'you aren't quite so good as you thought you were, Miss Gypsy,—you wanted to make out that you had seen it, though we hadn't.'

'Hush, boys, I daresay she thought she had seen it'; and turning to the little girl Miss Gubbins added, 'You mustn't think too much about the things I read to you, or I shall have to stop. You were dreaming last night so much that I suppose you fancied it was real, and that was what made yhu leave your bed this morning, I expect.'

Gypsy said no more, for her feelings were deeply wounded. She was a very truthful child, and to have her word doubted was a great trial. She had been so happy after her morning experience, so sure that the boys would believe her, and so delighted to be able to tell them of it, that it was a bitter disappointment to her to bear their scoffs and ridicule. The disappearance of the room was a great puzzle to her, and for the next few days she spent many hours in fruitless efforts to find it. She never mentioned the subject again, though the boys often teased her about it.; but one afternoon Miss Gubbins came into the nursery, or schoolroom, as it was now called, and found the little maiden at the window talking in low, vehement tones to her doll. Gypsy's doll was never in her arms unless she was in trouble of some sort. When she quarrelled with the boys, or was punished for some naughtiness, 'Helen Mary' was her comforter. And Miss Gubbins now wondered what had disturbed her mind. These were the words she heard.

'God will make them believe me on the judgment day. Gubby told us everything will be put right then. And He will tell them that I spoke the truth, the straight real truth, and that He sent me the Holy Thing Himself. Yes, He will, Helen Mary, and the boys will be all wrong, and I shall be quite, quite right!'

CHAPTER IV

A Crippled Knight

MISS GUBBINS had a difficult time for those first few weeks in the old house, and she longed for the advent of the master. Mrs. Peck ruled the household with a rod of iron. The old butler, Smythe by name, was her abject slave. He was a kind old man, and took a great fancy to the children, but his kindness was shown only in Mrs. Peck's absence. He would call them into his pantry, and give them all kinds of dainties such as children love, but let but the silk dress of Mrs. Peck rustle by, and he would drive them out in surly fright, muttering as he did so: 'Away with you, ye young plagues, a-comin' and a-worryin' round and a-drivin' a body nearly crazy!'

Mrs. Peck did not like children, and made no secret of her dislike to them. Perhaps, if they had been more docile and respectful to her, she would not have been so hard on them. As it was, there was perpetual contention between them, and Miss Gubbins could not keep the peace. Miss Gubbins herself was preoccupied and absorbed. The old house appealed to her poetic feelings, and she would wander through the empty rooms saying to herself:

'We have gone back a century here. No reminders

of the prosaic age in which we live, except the post and newspapers.'

And with her poetry-books in hand she dreamed away her days, only subject to rude awakenings by the incivility and neglect of the housekeeper, and the mischief and scrapes of her pupils.

Donald and Claud were enjoying themselves as they had never done before, and their imaginations were busy from morning to night planning tournaments and games of all kinds. There were as many resources indoors as out of doors, and most of the servants enjoyed hearing the merry shouts and laughter echoing through the house. The old coachman, Mills, declared sourly that they had 'destroyed his peace of mind for evermore'; but there was cause for such a speech after he was fetched out by the young groom to see each of the boys mounted on one of the fat old carriage-horses, with long poles in their hands, and tearing up the smooth gravel drive in front of the house by charging one another in the orthodox knightly fashion.

'We're King Arthur's knights, Mills; stand out of the way, or we'll ride you down!'

And it was some time before Mills could rescue his beloved horses from the hands of such fiery young warriors.

One afternoon Miss Gubbins was lying down with a bad headache, and the children had the schoolroom to themselves. Donald and Gypsy were perched on the top of the large square table, and Claud was seated on the old window-seat, making a boat out of a piece of wood, and watching the other two furtively, and rather disconsolately.

The table was a desert island, Donald was Robinson

Crusoe, and Gypsy his man Friday; the carpet had turned into a raging sea, chairs and stools were crocodiles and fish of all sorts, and with a hooked walking-stick Donald was hoisting various articles on to the island.

'I'll be a cannibal king, and come across to you in a boat,' suggested Claud presently.

'We don't want you; there's no room on the table for three,' said Donald. 'You wouldn't be Friday, and Gypsy makes a much better Friday, because she does what she is told.'

'I don't want to get on your old island,' said Claud crossly. Then after a minute, very persuasively:

'I could make a lovely earthquake under the table; you could be swaying and falling and clinging hold of the rocks——'

'We don't want an earthquake. Now, Friday, my gun; lie down; let me put my foot on you to take aim. I see a bear on a crocodile's back.'

Claud hacked away at his piece of wood with a clouded brow. At last he jumped up.

'This is a stupid old house!' he announced. 'I wish we were back at the sea; we always had heaps of children to play with there, and I shall go out and see if there aren't any about here. I shall find some one to play with.'

He took up his straw hat and marched off; the other two were so engrossed in their game that they did not notice his disappearance.

When tea-time came, and Miss Gubbins came out of her room, refreshed by her rest, no Claud was to be found. She was not alarmed, and it was not till it was nearly the children's bed-time that she began to make inquiries.

'He's run away,' suggested Gypsy cheerfully. 'He said he liked the seaside best; p'raps he's gone back there.'

'Have you been quarrelling again?'

'No; but we didn't want him, and he went away to play by himself.'

Miss Gubbins went downstairs out into the garden and round the stables with a worried face. When she asked Mills if he had seen him, the old man gave an indignant snort.

'Seed him! 'Tis the only blessed time in my life when I don't see any of 'em; but such times is rare indeed! 'Afore five o'clock in the mornin' they're always shoutin' and a tearin' round, and just where you last expec's to see 'em, there they'll sure to be. And if my 'pinion is axed, he's most likely took up by the perleece for robbin' orchards, or climbin' over genlemen's garden-walls, to pick whatever he can lay his hands on, and sauce and mock his elders and betters, if they do but say a rummonstratin' word!'

Then Miss Gubbins went through the grounds and out into the high road down to the little village, about a mile distant, Donald and Gypsy following her, and making anything but reassuring suggestions.

'He had a boat he was making. He's found the sea somewhere, and tumbled in and got drowned!'

'He's climbed a tree to get a rook's nest, and fallen down and broken both his legs!'

'He's lost his way in a wood, and got caught in a trap!' and so on, till Miss Gubbins hushed them rather sharply. Only one person in the village seemed to have seen him, and that was the baker's wife.

'The little fair-haired chap? Yes; I seed him a trottin' through the street this afternoon, and he were a talkin' to hisself like mad. He went straight along the road, and he hasn't come back to my knowledge.'

'That's Claud!' exclaimed Donald. 'He always talks to himself when he isn't pleased. Come on, Gubby, we shall find him.'

It was getting dark now, and Miss Gubbins was most uneasy. Not one of the servants had offered to search for her missing pupil, and she felt helpless and hopeless. At length, coming towards them along the dusty road, they spied a cart, and as it came nearer a little form in it jumped up, and throwing up his arms shouted out :

'Hulloo, Gubby! Here I am! And I've had such fun.'

It was Claud. The good-natured baker, coming back very late from his round, had overtaken a little tired, dusty figure plodding along, and recognising who it was, had lifted him into his cart and brought him back.

When Miss Gubbins found him safe and well she almost cried, the relief was so great, and Donald and Gypsy danced round him in the greatest excitement.

'Where have you been? What have you seen? Did you lose yourself? Mrs. Peck said she hoped you had, to give you a lesson. Tell us what you've been doing!'

But Claud, revelling in his importance now, pursed up his mouth and refused to say a word till he had got home and had had a good supper. Then his tongue was unloosed.

'I went out for a walk to find some children,' he said, 'and I peeped into three gardens on the road, and I asked a gardener about them, and he said no gentlefolk's children—that's what he called them—lived nearer than a white house high up on a hill that he showed me, and he said there were two there, only they were away from home ; and then I left him, and I saw a farm across some fields, and I thought I'd like to go and see the inside of it. And when I got up, one side of the house was all a dirty yard, with pigs and fowls and cows, and the other side was a jolly garden with a lot of grass and apple trees at the bottom, and there was a window opening right out on the grass, and when I got up I saw—guess ! '

' A lovely tea-table with cakes and buns, and a nice little girl in the middle of it,' suggested Gypsy.

' Two cross old ladies with a cat and a dog,' guessed Donald.

' You're both wrong. It was a man, and he was on a sofa, and over his legs was a lovely wolf-skin, with a wolf's head, and tongue, and teeth showing, and long claws to his feet, and no one else was in the room except the man, and he was drawing a picture, an awfully funny one. And when he saw me he said, " Halloo, youngster, have you dropped from the moon ? " And so then I pretended I had, and then he laughed out, and told me to come in, for he said he was longing for some one to talk to. And I told him I was wanting some one to play with, and he said he knew some lovely games, and he taught me one on paper, about a fox and a goose. I'll show you to-morrow.'

Claud stopped for breath, and Donald eagerly demanded, ' Did he give you anything to eat ? '

' Yes ; a huge slice of cake out of a cupboard. He said he had an old aunt who loved him so much, and spoilt him so much, and talked, and wrapped him up so much, that he was obliged to

run away from her every summer, because if he
didn't, he would turn into a stuffed old image that
could only nod and smile, with nothing to think
about but kittens' illnesses, and flannel petticoats
for old women! He was very funny, and I liked him.'

'And what else?' asked Gypsy. 'Did he shoot
the wolf that was over his legs? And what was he
lying on a sofa for?'

'He's got something the matter with his legs, and
he can't walk. He got lost on a mountain in the
rain, and he was very ill, and he's a cripple, he says.
He didn't seem to mind; he is staying there because
his nurse lives there. I asked him if he was a
nursery boy when he was little, and he said yes,
and fancy! he had a father and mother and four
brothers and sisters, and now they're all dead!'

'Who killed them?' asked Gypsy quickly.

'God did, I suppose,' was Claud's reply. Then
after a pause he went on, 'I told him I would come
and see him again. He can tell lovely stories, and
I think he likes some one to listen to them. He
has a chair on wheels, and he wheels himself out on
the grass, and he says he feels like an old cow
sometimes, because he has nothing to do but to
munch his food, look up at the blue sky, and move
round and round inside a small field, and to-day is
always the same as yesterday, and to-morrow will
be like to-day. I told him our days were never the
same, and then he listened, and I talked, and when
I was tired it was nearly dark, and so I came
away.'

'And now you are going to bed,' said Miss Gubbins, 'and you must never run away again without
telling me where you're going.'

Claud went off to bed obediently, but when Donald was half asleep, an hour later, he was awakened by his brother's call—

'Donald, look here; a man without legs can never be a knight, can he? Not a knight like King Arthur's?'

Donald rubbed his eyes.

'Don't bother!'

'Well, but just say. Would Arthur have had a cripple man, however brave he was?'

'Of course he wouldn't.'

'Then my friend can't play that with us. I wish he could.'

'Gubby said one of them got tired, and turned monk,' murmured Donald. 'Don't you remember?'

'Yes, I know; it was the one who told the story of Galahad. What was his name? Oh, I know, Sir Perceval. And that's what I shall call my friend. He wouldn't tell me his name—at least, he said it was "Bob Bogus." That's what he puts at the bottom of his pictures—the funny ones I told you about. He sends them to *Punch*. But that isn't his real name, and Sir Perceval is much nicer.'

A grunt was Donald's only response, and Claud turned over on his pillow, seeing further conversation was useless. But as he, too, drifted into dreamland, he murmured, 'A legless knight could be brave, I am sure.'

It was not long before Claud visited his friend again. He slipped away quietly from the others at play, and confided in Miss Gubbins alone where he was going.

'You see, Gubby, I don't want them to come with me. He's my friend, not theirs, and Donald doesn't think much of him because his legs are all wrong.'

'I don't know whether you ought to visit strangers so,' said Miss Gubbins, hesitating. 'Still, your brother will be here soon, and he can settle questions of that kind. Only don't come home late. You must be in time for tea.'

Away trotted Claud. It was not very far, now he knew the way. He crept round to the front of the house facing the apple orchard, and there he saw, to his delight, the wheeled chair under the shade of an apple-tree.

Claud marched up with a radiant face.

'Good afternoon, Sir Perceval,' he said, holding out his hand.

His friend started, and glanced up surprised at his new title. He was quite a young man, and rather a handsome one. His was a face that knew how to suffer and be strong, and perhaps the weary, sad look about his blue eyes was the only indication that he had known trouble. There was no sadness in tone or look as he exclaimed—

'Since when have I been knighted, may I ask?'

'Oh, I've knighted you myself. Gubby read us and told us about Sir Perceval, who left King Arthur and went into a monk's house to be quiet and good; at least the others were just as good, I'm sure, only I thought you'd do to be him, because you can't ride in tournaments.'

'Thanks. I will answer to my name. May I prove worthy of it! When does the next tournament come off? Tell me some news of King Arthur's Court. I have been so long away from it that I've forgotten the manners and customs of it.'

'We've been looking busily for the Holy Thing,' said Claud, settling himself down on the grass and gazing up at the newly-made knight with shining eyes. 'You saw it, didn't you, as well as Galahad? only you weren't quite good enough to be caught away like he was.'

The young man looked at the little speaker rather thoughtfully.

'Oh—ah, the Holy Grail, I remember; though it is years since I read it. Yes, you're right, though you don't know how near I was to being caught away a year or so ago. As you say, I " wasn't quite good enough!"'

Then Claud relapsed into everyday talk.

'Yes, and there's Gypsy actually, who is always in mischief quite as bad as Donald and me, she pretends and sticks to it that she really did—honour bright—see the Holy Thing in a strange kind of church room in our house very early in the morning! And she says the room has disappeared. As if a girl would be good enough to see it!'

'I think a girl was the first one to see it. Wasn't it Sir Perceval's sister, the nun?'

'Oh, well, she was a grown-up person. Not a creature like Gypsy!'

'And what is this despised Gypsy like? A nut-brown maid?'

'No, she isn't brown; her hair is like mine, and always untidy, and she has only just given up wearing socks, and she's never still a minute.'

'Poor little maiden! Do you think you are more likely to catch sight of it than she is?'

'I'm not very good myself,' said Claud reflectively. 'I don't think any of us are. Don and I try to be knights whenever we get a chance, and now we're in a proper kind of castle we feel much more like them. Then you see the Ogre will be coming back soon, and all kinds of things will happen. He is our grown-up brother—we call him the Ogre because he has a great moustache, which he pulls when he is angry, and he is a big, tall man, and I think he means to be very cruel to us when he comes back. At least we pretend he is going to be. It's more fun, you see!'

'We'll hope he won't disappoint you.'

They chatted on, and when Claud left his friend an hour after, he said by way of farewell:

'I dare say I'll come and see you pretty often. I suppose you can't ever come and see us? Gubby would ask you to tea, if you could get up the stairs.'

'Thanks, but I'm afraid my old legs couldn't do it. I tell them sometimes they've done their best to make me a decrepit old man, but I've got a little friend who won't let them have all their own way. He keeps them from worrying me.'

'Who is he?'

'Ah, well, he has a variety of names. He is a little companion of mine, and helps me to do my sketches. Good-bye, and bring that little sister of yours to see me next time you come.'

'Good-bye, Sir Perceval.'

CHAPTER V

The ' Ogre's ' Arrival

IT was a wet day. Lessons had been done; dinner was over, and Miss Gubbins had told her little charges not to leave the schoolroom. She had been reading them some of the *Idylls of the King*; and then seeing them settle down quietly on the old window-seat to talk them over, she slipped away to write some letters in her room. The servants were all busy making preparations for their master, as he was now expected back any day, and Mrs. Peck was in the worst of humours, scolding the maids, and full of lamentation over the old times that were gone.

The children wisely kept out of her way; even Smythe would have nothing to do with them, and they were glad to have the safe refuge of the schoolroom to play in.

Now they were talking with serious eyes, and in earnest tones, about their beloved King Arthur and his knights.

'I'll be Arthur,' said Donald, at last starting up, 'and I'm going to give a banquet to Launcelot and my queen. Come on to the table!'

'It isn't like Arthur's table,' objected Claud, 'it's a nasty square thing, and you're not to sit at the head of it, Don, for Arthur never had a head, he sat equal with his knights!'

'Couldn't we pretend it was round?' suggested Gypsy.

Donald walked round the offending object with frowning brow, then his face cleared.

'We'll make it round,' he said; 'we'll cut off the corners!'

Claud capered up and down with delight at this inspiration.

'With our pocket-knives! Come on!'

The table was an old mahogany one, and the boys found it harder work than they anticipated.

'Will Gubby be angry?' asked Gypsy doubtfully, as she saw the shavings drop on the carpet.

'She knows we like a round table,' said Donald, panting for breath, as he hacked away with a ruthless hand. 'I know what will be better. I will go and get a saw. There is one in the toolhouse.'

Away he ran, and Claud rested from his labour.

'You see,' he explained to Gypsy, who was looking on with round eyes, 'it's a very old table, and it's covered with ink, and it always has a cloth on, so it can't be very wrong to make it round instead of square!'

Donald soon returned, and the destruction of the table was renewed with fresh vigour. They were in the very midst of it, when the door suddenly opened, and Victor Thurston stood on the threshold.

So intent had they been in their occupation that his arrival, and the consequent bustle in the house, had been entirely unnoticed by them. It was an unfortunate meeting.

A short, sharp ejaculation started the children. 'Good heavens, what imps of mischief! Where on earth is your governess? Does she allow you to hack all the furniture to pieces in this fashion?'

D

Gypsy ran out of the room thoroughly frightened ; Claud retreated to the window-seat ; Donald only stood his ground.

'We're only altering our table a little. We want it round. This is our table, and this is our room, Mrs. Peck said so!'

He looked defiant, as he often did when his conscience told him he had done wrong ; but the hurried entrance of Miss Gubbins, and her horror-stricken exclamations and apologies cut his excuses short.

'You must have your hands full,' said Victor, with a short laugh, as he tried to greet Miss Gubbins politely, 'if this is a specimen of how they employ themselves in your absence!'

'They have never done such a naughty thing before,' said poor Miss Gubbins. 'I cannot think how they could have dared to do it! Come and tell your brother how sorry you are, Donald, for spoiling his furniture so!'

'It isn't his table, it's ours,' muttered Donald sullenly.

'Look here, youngster,' and Victor drew his little brother to him by the ear. 'I have given you a home here, but I don't expect you to ruin everything in it by wanton mischief. You are old enough to know better. We'll say no more about it now, but don't let me find you destroying anything else, or there will be a row. Now make yourself scarce, for I want to have a few words with Miss Gubbins.'

Donald darted out of the room, and Claud followed him.

Victor looked after them ; then with a smile and shrug of his shoulders, said to Miss Gubbins, 'I hope I have not made a mistake in having them here. I

never pretend to understand children; they are un-
known quantities to me, but I wanted to give them a
comfortable home, and I was going to ask you, Miss
Gubbins, if you felt it possible to superintend the household here a little. They say it wants a lady to make
a place homelike, and these old servants have had it
all their own way too long. I thought perhaps I
could make some arrangement about the boys being
taught out of the house, if only for a few hours every
day, and Gypsy seems such a baby that she would
not require much of your time. What do you think?
Of course it remains with you whether you would be
willing to try it.'

Miss Gubbins gazed out of the window with a little
frown between her eyes. She took off her *pince-nez*,
rubbed them nervously, then put them on, and looked
up at the young man before her.

'I will be quite frank with you,' she said. 'I could
not superintend such a large household and the children's lessons too. If the boys were taken off my
hands it would be a different matter; but even then,
unless you gave Mrs. Peck notice to leave, I should
not like to attempt it. She does not like our being
here, and would never be willing to take any orders
from me.'

'Mrs. Peck can go to Jericho!' exclaimed Victor,
a little hotly; 'she treated me to a little of her inde-
pendence directly I came into the house. I wrote to
her to make you thoroughly comfortable; I find she
has banished you to the top of the house, and when I
remonstrated, I met with quiet insolence. One thing
I have quite determined, and that is, to be master
here; and the sooner she knows it, and every one else
too, the better it will be for them all!'

Miss Gubbins was silent. Victor went on:

'I shall lead a very quiet life here; there is a good bit of land which will need my attention, and I shall be in town very often. I want things to go on smoothly in my absence, and I don't consider Mrs. Peck will be needed any more. The cook, I find, has been here fifteen years, and seems a motherly, capable old body, quite anxious to escape Mrs. Peck's rule. Don't decide hastily, but let me know in a day or two what you feel about it. I won't keep you any longer now, but I hope you will dine with me at eight to-night. I conclude the children will be in bed by that time, and if not, there are plenty of servants here to look after them.'

He strode away, and Miss Gubbins heaved a heavy sigh. 'I must do it. I don't mind the house-keeping. It is these old servants I dread, and I shall not like to lose control over the boys. I hope they will get on well with Mr. Thurston. I wish he were not quite so masterful.'

And then with another sigh she settled herself in the window-seat, and took up one of her beloved poets to soothe her perturbed spirit.

The children meanwhile were discussing the arrival of their brother with vigour, in a favourite corner of theirs on the stairs. It was a little square landing overlooking the entrance hall, and was partially curtained off the wide staircase.

If 'Agony's' subjects proved rebellious, she was sure to rush out at them from this corner after dusk as they passed upstairs, and Gypsy passed the heavy damask curtain at all times with awe and dread. She was sitting now on the floor, her legs well tucked under her, and Donald was holding forth:

'He's a worse Ogre than ever, and he'll make this house a kind of prison. He pinched my ear till I could have kicked him! He thinks he is going to be a kind of lord here.'

'Like King Arthur,' put in Gypsy; 'and we shall be the knights, only we don't love him like they loved Arthur!'

'I've just made up my mind what I shall do,' said Claud, sticking his hands in his pockets, and his chin in the air; 'I shall get one of those suits of armour off the wall, and dress up in one, and I shall go to his bedroom at night, and frighten him well!'

'You'd be a wicked boy, then,' said Gypsy, who had a fellow feeling for any one frightened after dark, 'and perhaps you'd make him into an idiot, like the boy that Gubby told us about!'

'We'll do it, Claud,' said Donald with enthusiasm, 'and we'll do it to-morrow night!'

'And then he'll take out his pistol and shoot you,' pursued Gypsy; 'and it will serve you right, for Arthur's knights never went about frightening people. Galahad wouldn't do it.'

'I'm not going to be Galahad,' said Donald, a little impatiently, 'he was too good. I can't be good, so it's no use trying.'

'Then you'll never see the Holy Thing.'

'Well, you won't, so you needn't think it. You're not a bit better than we are; you're worse, for you're a girl, and girls are made to be good, and Jane says you kicked her this morning!'

'Well,' said Gypsy, a little abashed, 'she tried to shut me into a cupboard "to keep me quiet," she said. I was only just getting a blacking brush to clean Helen Mary's shoes, and it was only a tiny little soft kick on her dress! I told her I was sorry after, because I'm trying hard to find the Holy Thing!'

The boys did not listen to this defence; they were busily engaged in laying their plans for the next night. They had both a great longing to get down one of the suits of armour from the wall, and try it on, but the difficulty was to reach them. However, the next day they pressed Ned, the stable-boy, into their service, and when Miss Gubbins went down to dine with their brother, the three conspirators crept to the darkest corner of the big hall, and with great trouble the smallest suit of armour was unfastened, and Claud put into it. The weight of it astonished and alarmed him.

'I'm nearly buried,' he said in a muffled voice; 'I can't keep it on long, Don. Let me out!'

'No; you must come upstairs and hide in his bed-room, and wait till he comes to bed!'

'That will be hours and hours; it's so heavy; I can't wait all that time!'

After further consideration they decided that Claud should hide in 'Agony's' corner on the stairs, and pounce out upon his victim as he came upstairs. It was a great labour to help him up there, but that was accomplished at last, and then Donald ran up to tell Gypsy that everything was in readiness. The auda-city of the exploit awed her, but though she felt in her small heart that trouble would follow, she could not resist creeping out of bed and down the stairs to see Claud in his armour.

'Oh,' she said with clasped hands, 'you look beau-tiful, Claud, dear.'

'It's awful hot and uncomfortable,' was Claud's response.

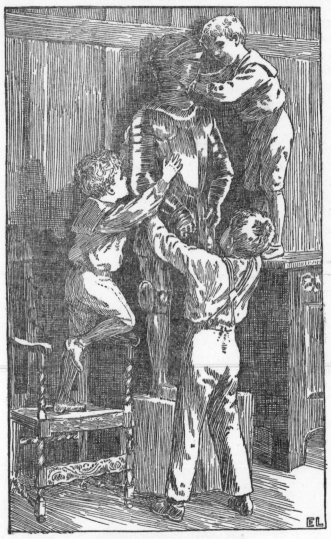

THE ARMOUR WAS UNFASTENED.

'Yes, but just think! You're like a real knight now, and no one would be able to hurt you, if you had a fight. Who do you feel like? Galahad or Launcelot?'

'Sh—sh! Here's some one coming!' cried Donald. Away he and Gypsy scampered back to their beds, and Claud stepped behind the curtain.

It was only Miss Gubbins. Having left Victor to have a smoke, she was coming up to her own set of rooms. Claud held his breath while she went by. Though he was sorely tempted to show himself, he refrained from doing so, as he knew in that case his plan would be frustrated. Time passed very slowly. Donald and Gypsy did not return to him, and his shoulders and arms were aching from the heavy weight of his armour. 'It isn't much fun, after all,' was his rueful thought; and then at last he heard his brother's voice in the hall, and the quick, heavy tread up the staircase.

Opening the curtain, he strode out.

'Who goes there?'

The challenge was not given in such gruff, manly tones as was planned. If truth must out, it was a very thin quavering treble squeak, and Victor was not in the least alarmed. For a minute he stood still, regarding the queer little figure in front of him with some amusement; then in a very determined tone he said:

'This will never do. I can't have my old armour walking over the house in this style. I must string it up again, and drive a nail through the helmet to make it secure.'

Before Claud knew where he was, he found himself tucked under Victor's arm and being carried downstairs as if he were a mere parcel.

He was too proud to call out, and the rapid movement through the air so bewildered him that it was not till he fancied he actually felt a cord being tied round his neck, and expected to be slung up on the wall the next minute, that all his courage deserted him.

Then Victor heard a piteous little muffled cry out of the old visor :

'Oh, please let me out! I won't do it again, I promise! Please undo me, and let me go out!'

But Victor was not so easily persuaded.

'I'll tie you up here, whoever you are, and there you shall stay till I choose to release you.'

Poor Claud found he was being secured effectually to an old stone pillar in the outer hall, and then, whistling unconcernedly, his step-brother pursued his way upstairs, and he was left alone in the darkness.

This was turning the tables on him with a vengeance! The servants' hall was too far off to hear his muffled cries for help ; he ached from the heavy, cumbersome weight of the armour, and he longed with all his heart to be safe in his own little bed. He wondered if Donald would come to his rescue, but he would not think of looking for him downstairs, and poor Claud quite expected to be left there all night.

It seemed to be hours to him before he saw, through the dimly-lighted hall, the figure of his brother descending the stairs.

But he was liberated at last, and emerged from his knightly covering, a tearful, woe-begone little figure.

'Now off to bed with you, and let this be the last prank with any of the armour here !'

Claud crept up to bed, quite cured of his love of intimidating any 'grown up,' but with less love than ever for the one who had outdone him.

CHAPTER VI

A Great Disappointment

CHANGES were rapidly made after the young master had come home, but Mrs. Peck was not got rid of without a terrible struggle, and Miss Gubbins had to leave her poetry books and brace herself for the conflict. She was victor at last, for she was backed up by the 'master'; but it ended in five or six of the other servants giving notice, and only Smythe and the cook remained of the old set. Being so busy with these household difficulties gave her less time than ever to look after the children, and they practically 'ran wild,' as the saying is. Victor still figured as the 'Ogre,' and was shunned accordingly; but the house was big and empty enough to furnish pastime away from him, and they did not trouble him with their noise. Claud introduced Gypsy and Donald one afternoon to 'Sir Perceval,' and they all agreed that he was the 'very funniest, jolliest fellow' they had ever seen.

'So you're the little lady who has seen the Holy Grail?' he asked Gypsy, just before the children were taking their departure.

Gypsy drew near to the wheeled chair with soft, serious blue eyes.

'Yes, I really and truly did see it,' she said steadfastly; 'and I'm trying hard to be very good enough to see it again.'

'I suppose you had been awfully good just before you saw it?'

'I don't think I was very,' admitted Gypsy doubtfully, 'but I got up very early in the morning to look for it; it says so, you know!'

The boys had moved off, interested in the antics of a young foal just outside the orchard, and Gypsy felt she could speak quite freely to this pleasant-faced young man.

'Does it?' her questioner said doubtfully, taking up a volume of Tennyson that he had been referring to during the children's visit. 'I think it was chiefly seen at night.'

'It says, "Those that seek Me early shall find Me,"' pursued Gypsy; 'the lady said I ought to be looking for Jesus, and I should find Him, and the Holy Thing belongs to Him, doesn't it? If you see it, that means you must be getting near Jesus. And I knelt down and said my prayers, and then I saw the Holy Thing, just like Gubby told us. A rose red light, and yellow, it came down right on me; and the boys say I'm telling stories, and it's the straight real truth!'

'Sir Perceval' gazed at the little speaker in astonishment, and a softened expression stole over his face.

'I thought I had found a little mystic who loved fairy stories,' he said slowly; 'but I've found a mite who is searching for the deepest truth on earth, ay, and in heaven itself! Seeking for the Lord Jesus Christ are you, little one?'

Gypsy nodded. 'I'm wanting to find Him. If you're very very good, I think He shows Himself to you just for a little minute, and I would so like to see Him!'

Her little mouth took wistful curves as she spoke, and for a moment there was silence.

'And what do you want to see Him for?'

'I should like Him to tell me He loved me, and was pleased with me, and would let me come to heaven when I die! I think I might have seen Him another day, because I found the right room, but I've lost it, and it seems to have gone, and no one knows anything about it!'

Then after another pause, she asked eagerly:

'Have you ever seen or heard Jesus, Sir Perceval?'

'Sir Perceval's' face was very grave now. All the sparkle had died out of his eyes.

'I did hear Him once,' he said thoughtfully.

'Oh, how nice! And did you see the Holy Thing?'

He shook his head, then turned to look after the boys.

'We're getting into deep water,' he said lightly, 'and you're looking as grave as a judge. Don't you know that children ought always to be crying or laughing, and a solemn face is never allowed until you're grown up and married!'

Gypsy walked home thoughtfully between the two boys. The longing to find her quest took a strong possession of her, and after the schoolroom tea was over that afternoon, again she wandered down the old passages, trying every door, in the hope of coming across the one she wanted.

She was much startled and delighted when at last, opening one door, she found herself on the threshold of the lost room.

There was the beautiful coloured window; the walls lined with books; the large square table in the

GYPSY TRIES THE DOOR.

middle of the room, but, seated writing at this table was the Ogre!

For a moment the child hesitated, then her curiosity overcame her shyness, and she advanced with a radiant face.

Victor looked up and wondered at the intrusion.

'How did you find this room out?' he asked, a little impatiently. 'I thought I was safe here from all disturbance. This room is not for you children. Run away!'

The gladness died out of Gypsy's face at once, but she stood her ground.

'You aren't going to keep it all to yourself?' she asked with vehemence. 'It's the room I found and lost, and it's the room which the Holy Thing is in. I want to see it again, and the boys want to see it too, and they'll know I wasn't telling stories when they see it!'

Victor stared at her, and wondered what had wrought up her feelings to such a pitch that she could stand her ground before him, instead of running away directly she saw him, as was her custom.

'What on earth are you talking about?' he asked, laying down his pen, and leaning back in his chair with a yawn. 'What is the " Holy Thing," may I ask ?'

'You know. Haven't you seen it ? It's what Sir Galahad saw, and what all Arthur's knights looked for, and I thought p'raps we should find it in this house, and I found it all by myself early in the morning, and it came through that window up there!'

Her words still were absolutely unintelligible to him.

'What came through the window ?'

'The Holy Thing. That's what we call it. Gubby calls it the Holy Grail, and Don says it's the Holy Light ; but I saw it, and I want to see it again.'

Dimly he began to understand, and he looked at his little sister with some interest.

'You don't mean to tell me that you harum-scarum youngsters are playing at such a game as searching for the Holy Grail ? Can you carry your imaginations and pretences so far as to believe in it yourself, I wonder ?'

'I don't understand. It wasn't pretence. It was real truth, and the Holy Thing came down on my head. I saw it. It fell on my fingers and dress.'

The earnestness and intensity of her tone amused him.

'You are queer little creatures,' he said ; 'but I can't have you romping in this old library ; it is generally locked up, and I use it but seldom.'

'But let me, oh, please let me come in here early in the morning ! I will be very good. I won't touch a thing. I'll just come in like I did before, and kneel down and say my prayers, and then, perhaps, I shall see it again.'

Victor laughed, and turned to his writing.

'Well, if you want to turn it into a private chapel for your devotions, I don't suppose you can do much harm, but no romps or games in it, remember, and when I'm using it, make yourself scarce. Now run along, and leave me in peace.'

Gypsy instantly obeyed, and fled along the passage in trembling delight, calling out :

'Don! Claud! I've found it!'

The boys were so engrossed in letting themselves up and down over the banisters by means of a rope they had tied to the top rail, that they did not respond to their sister's call.

It was not till Miss Gubbins came out and forbade their fascinating occupation, and sent them all into the schoolroom to be quiet till tea-time, that Gypsy obtained a hearing. Then the boys were interested in it at once.

Where is the room? Did you see the Holy Thing?'

'Of course she didn't if the Ogre was there; he would frighten anything away.'

'We'll go and see it directly after tea.'

'No,' said Gypsy gravely; 'he said we weren't to come in there while he was there; but to-morrow morning early, when he is in bed, we can go. And then you'll see I wasn't telling stories!'

'I don't believe we shall see it,' said Donald sceptically. 'I'm sure it's a make up of yours!'

'You won't see it unless you're very good,' said Gypsy diplomatically, 'and if you're cross and say I'm telling stories, you won't see it at all!'

'We'll just be as good as gold,' Claud said earnestly, 'until to-morrow morning, and then if it's all a pretend, you'll catch it hot.'

Miss Gubbins wondered a little at the quiet and peace that reigned in her small kingdom for the rest of the evening. The children sat on the low window seat, and talked in low tones, without the shadow of a dispute amongst them. They had hit upon the delightful plan of telling each other all the naughty things they might do, if they were not trying to be good, and all vied with one another in proving that their brain was the most fertile in concocting mischievous devices.

The only danger in this was, that they began to have a longing to put them into practice, and Donald wound up by saying :

' If we don't see the Holy Grail after all, it will be no use trying to be good any more, and then I shall just try a few of our plans.'

All this made little Gypsy very anxious. She felt as if great issues hung upon the early morning visit to the library, and for a long time that night tossed about restlessly in her sleep, until at last Miss Gubbins came over to soothe her.

' What is it, dear ? Is anything troubling you ? Have you had dreams ? '

Gypsy's flushed little face and disordered curls turned over on the pillow.

' If we don't see it, we shall never be good again, the boys say so.'

And Miss Gubbins crept back to bed, hoping that such a dreadful statement only existed in dreamland.

Very early the next morning Gypsy was in her brothers' room with shining eyes and eager face. It did not often fall to her lot to be leader, and she was a little proud, and very fearful of the responsibility attached to it.

E

The boys were up in a moment, and three little figures instead of one now stole down the long corridor and into the old library.

It was unlocked this time, though for one moment the stiffness of the door handle made Gypsy tremble lest after all they should not gain an entrance. But directly they stood inside her little heart was at rest. There through that wonderful window was the coloured light, and it fell full on their pathway in rays of crimson and gold. Awed and delighted, she turned in triumph to the boys, but no ecstatic joy shone in their faces.

With a broad grin Donald spoke, and his words ruthlessly shattered poor Gypsy's beautiful conception.

'Why, you little stupid! You don't think that's the Holy Grail? It's just the sun shining through the coloured glass! Just like a girl! Haven't you seen a painted window before? I have, in a church Gubby took me to once, and I remember it all shone over the clergyman, and gave him a red nose and a blue mouth ; he did look so funny ! '

'Fancy bringing us to see that, and telling us it was the Holy Thing !' said Claud contemptuously.

Poor little Gypsy ! Her face fell, and big tears began to gather in her blue eyes. She had been so happy, so sure of the vision, and now it was roughly taken away from her, and the boys, instead of being awed and solemnized, were laughing loudly at her stupidity. She stood immovable for a moment, and then, flinging herself down on the floor, gave way to a fit of bitter weeping. Her distress touched Donald's heart. He sat down by her and tried to comfort her.

'Don't be a cry-baby. Anyhow, you found out a